A POCKETFUL OF FUR

A Pocketful of Fur

by Deb Loughead

Illustrated by The Yelling Birke Sister

A Hodgepog Book

Hodgepog Books acknowledges the ongoing support of the Canada Council for the Arts and the B.C. Arts Council.

EDITORS
Luanne Armstrong and Dorothy Woodend.

COVER DESIGN AND INTERIOR LAYOUT
Jane Lightle, Bibelot Communications.
Set in AT Sackers and Adobe Garamond.

Published in Canada by Hodgepog Books,
3476 Tupper Street
Vancouver, BC V5Z 3B7
604.874.1167

NATIONAL LIBRARY OF CANADA CATALOGUING IN PUBLICATION DATA
Loughead, Deb
    Pocketful of Fur / Deb Loughead; Lisa Birke, illustrator. — New ed.

ISBN 0-9730831-6-6

I. Birke, Lisa II. Title.
PS8573.O8633P62 2003   jC813'.54   C2003-911250-0

Printed in Canada.

To my son, Alex, the middle one

ONE

"OUCH! My ear! Get lost, Matilda!" When I pushed the bird off my pillow, she flew up to the top of my closet door and sat there squawking at me. Then she cocked her head and peered at me with those beady little eyes of hers, like it was my fault that we'd all slept in and nobody had given her an orange slice yet.

"Dirty bird, dirty bird," she squawked.

"All right already," I squawked back at her. "I'm getting up, dirty bird!"

Not too many kids wake up in the morning with a cockatoo nibbling on their ear. Or a dog licking their face. Or a cat playing tag with their toes. Or a rabbit sniffing their cheek. Or on some days, all of the above! None of my friends do, that's for sure, but for some reason they all think I'm so lucky. Of course none of them have to live in a "zoo" like I do.

Buster and Chester were sleeping in my slippers, so I didn't bother putting them on. After all, how can a couple of kittens resist curling up in a pair of great big fluffy slippers shaped like bear paws? Riley, our goofy old golden mutt, followed me down to the kitchen, like he always does, clicking along behind me on the tiles, then patiently waiting at the back door until I let him out. And of course, Matilda came complaining through the air over my head, doing her best ringing telephone imitation as she landed on her perch in the kitchen to wait for her morning treat.

Those floor tiles were cold on my bare feet. My parents keep the furnace turned way down at night to conserve energy. And we can never have carpets in our house because of all the animals. It just wouldn't be sanitary, if you know what I mean. So even though it was early spring, I stood there freezing at the back door, waiting for Riley to finish doing his business.

Trixie, the kittens' mother, curled herself around my ankles, meowing for her breakfast. The reason we have five cats, is that when my Mom adopted Trixie from the animal shelter, she didn't realize that she was actually adopting a pregnant cat. Of course, she couldn't part with the kittens after she watched them being born, so we kept them all. A couple more were hanging around the house somewhere. Probably sleeping with my older sister Nicki.

The kitchen was quiet for a Saturday morning, which was unusual because my parents always get up with the birds. I mean literally. They like to get up and start bird watching early on Saturday morning. Every year they do this winter bird count for an ornithological society, and they have to keep track of every species that visits our feeders, from December until April. So it was odd that the coffee wasn't brewing, and the newspapers weren't rattling, and that the collection of animals that we live with wasn't already fed.

I was thinking about all this as I dumped food into the various bowls and started to peel an orange for squawking Matilda. That's when I heard the garage door opening, the thumping of boots, and some very enthusiastic voices.

"Max! You're up! Good morning!" My Mom emerged from the mud room, her cheeks rosy with the cold. She was dressed for the Arctic even though it was the beginning of April.

"Good morning, good morning, good morning," Matilda said, then flew over and landed on Mom's toque.

"Can I at least get my hat and coat off before you start pestering me, Matilda," Mom said. But she said it in a voice that meant she didn't mind, the same gentle voice that she uses to speak to all our animals. She carried Matilda over to her perch and started to feed her the orange.

"So where were you guys?" I asked as I poured myself a bowl of cereal. Dad answered me as he came stomping up from the mud room behind Mom.

"It's migration season," he said. "We were down at the lake with all our birder friends, checking out some of the species that are passing through on the way up north."

"Then," Mom continued, "we stopped by this construction site where they've chopped down an incredible stand of old oak trees. I'm telling you Max, it brought tears to my eyes. It's so pointless and destructive." She actually wiped a tear from the corner of her eye. Anything that has to do with nature makes my mom cry. You should see her when Bambi's mother dies!

"But one good thing came of it," Dad said.

"And what's that?" I asked with a sudden feeling of dread.

"This!" Dad plunged his hand deep into his coat pocket.

I held my breath. One good thing usually means an addition to our rapidly growing family.

"Whoops!" Dad said. "He's squirming around. I can't get a good grip on him."

Oh oh, I thought as my stomach plummeted to my feet. "A good grip on what, Dad?" I asked him, trying my best to sound enthusiastic.

"On this, Max," he said, and triumphantly held out a handful of fur.

"And what exactly is that, Dad," I said, but he didn't have to answer, because in another second it was sitting up on its tiny haunches, staring at me as curiously as I was staring back. It was a squirrel, the teeniest one I'd ever seen.

"Poor little baby," Mom said, touching it gently between the ears. "We figure he got separated from his family when all the trees were felled. He was just running around in circles at the construction site, completely flustered. Who knows what would have happened to him if we hadn't come to the rescue."

"And look at the interesting colour combination in his fur. Sort of a mixture of grey and black. Very unique, don't you think, Max?" Dad said.

I stood there staring at my parents who were gushing over that squirrel like it was a new baby or something.

"Not another animal," I said. Then I spun around and stomped out of the kitchen, leaving the whole weird menagerie behind. It would have been an incredibly dramatic exit, too, if I hadn't tripped over old Tom the tortoise in the hallway and fallen flat on my face. Which made me stomp even harder going up the stairs to my bedroom.

Okay, so I wasn't thrilled. But it isn't easy living in a house full of animals. Especially when your parents are these new-age hippies who were born too late and missed out on the whole 1960's flower-child experience, so are somehow trying to make up for it. I mean, some days I feel like I'm the one who's the parent in our house.

I lay there on my bed, brooding about everything that bugged me. For one thing, I could never bring friends over to our place. Well, I guess I could, but it's just that I was a little embarrassed about the smell. Sometimes, walking through our front door smells a lot like walking into a barn. It's not that our house isn't clean. My parents are careful about taking care of their animals. The litter boxes are always fresh, the papers on the bottom of Matilda's cage get changed every day, and the dogs (we actually have two of them; the other's a mini-dachshund named Otto) are shampooed at least once a month. But there's just no denying that unmistakable animal odour that fills up a house.

My sister and I don't always have clean laundry, either, and we have to fend for ourselves most of the time, since our parents are often at one protest or another supporting their environmental causes, when they aren't at work. And the house itself isn't always the tidiest. Stuff is usually strewn around, and every now and then we do this pick-up blitz to get it back in shape. So it's a pretty different lifestyle at the Harper homestead. And not one you want open for inspection by your friends, who might not understand.

As I was lying there brooding about all this stuff, there was a tiny knock on my door. It opened just a crack.

"Someone wants to get to know you better," a voice said. It was Mom. I watched the doorway as something dark and furry scurried into my bedroom. "We've named him Woodrow, because we found him in a wood row!"

"Woodrow the squirrel," I said. "Nifty name. But I'm calling him Woody."

"He's really very sweet," Mom said. "He thinks I'm his mother. I think he's imprinted on us already."

Imprinted. Those are the sort of words that my parents are always using. My mom figured she had already become a sort of surrogate mother to the squirrel. Lucky him! "That's nice," I said.

"Here." Mom held out her hand and trickled some sunflower seeds into my palm. "Try feeding him."

I held my hand out to Woody and he scrambled over and started nibbling on the seeds. His mini feet tickled my skin. After munching for a moment, he ran up my arm then sprang from my shoulder to my head and began kneading my hair. Mom sat on my bed, giggling like crazy.

"Oh Max, he's so cute. How can anyone resist a baby animal?"

I just rolled my eyes and sighed.

TWO

My parents rigged up a cage for Woody in the basement. It was an old parrot cage that my mom picked up at a garage sale, because it just might come in handy some day. After all, you never know when an animal emergency might come up. We have a great supply of empty cages cluttering up our garage. Everything from little gerbil cages with squeaky wheels, to huge terrariums large enough to hold a good-sized iguana.

Peter's rabbit cage was down in the basement, too. (How unique! A rabbit named Peter!) Only Peter always had the run, or should I say the 'hop' of the house. He was litter trained, and always went back to his cage to do his business. The rest of the time he was a free-range bunny. Just like old Tom the tortoise, you never knew where you'd find him.

I'd been tripping over Tom since I'd learned to walk. He was fifteen-years-old, three years older than me. Dad had given him to Mom as a wedding gift, believe it or not. Which just goes to show how crazy they are about animals.

At school on Monday, I didn't tell anyone about our new addition. Anyone except Blake, that is. Blake is my best friend, and I tell him everything. He's the only one who understands about the animals. And about the smell. On Monday morning, as usual, he'd saved a seat for me on the bus.

"Guess what," I told him as I flopped onto the seat beside him.

"What," Blake said, without looking up from the novel he was reading.

"We got another one."

That caught his attention fast. He looked over at me with wide eyes. Then he grinned.

"What kind is it this time?" he asked.

"A baby squirrel," I said.

"Cool!" Blake said. "I'm coming over to see it after school. And don't start whining and complaining to me either. You know how jealous I am about all your pets."

"Fine," I said, and bit back the grumble that was on the tip of my tongue. "But you wouldn't feel that way if you had to live at my house."

"Just try me," he said. "Anything's better than life in the sterile zone." The sterile zone. That's what Blake calls his house.

"Trade you," I said.

"Any day," Blake told me with a scowl.

Blake got off the school bus with me after school. We had to walk a couple of blocks to my house, and he was in such a hurry to meet Woody that he was practically jogging. But we had to slow down to a crawl when we caught up to Mrs. Baxter.

Mrs. Baxter lived across the street from us, in this huge old place that was probably a farmer's house a long time ago when our neighbourhood used to be farmland. Mrs. Baxter never spoke much to anybody, except maybe to murmur "hello," or "nice day, isn't it?" She always seemed to be wrapped up in her own little world, like she couldn't even hear you or something. To me she seemed to be about a hundred years old, but my mom told me that she was probably only in her seventies. Old Mrs. Baxter was one peculiar lady. She was doddering along the sidewalk when we caught up to her, watching her feet as she walked. Blake stopped in his tracks.

"Should we pass her?" he whispered to me. "Wouldn't it be rude?"

"Of course we should pass her," I said. "I do it all the time."

Blake and I slipped past her, and I mumbled excuse me the way I always do. And got no response, the way I never do. One peculiar lady.

"Someone told me she's a witch," Blake said as he zoomed along. I was out of breath trying to keep up with him. "That she's a bit strange or something."

"Who told you that?"

"Oh, some kid at school. She said she heard it from someone else, who heard it from their parents, who heard it from an uncle, who heard it from a shop owner."

"Sounds like the start of an urban legend," I told him. "But I doubt she's a witch. I mean, her place looks pretty spooky at times, with all those peaks and points on the roof. And the crows that roost in those big trees on her property, boy, when they start cawing and circling around her house, it's like a scene from a horror movie. But Mrs. Baxter is no witch. That's the dumbest thing I've ever heard."

I didn't want to mention the weird sounds I heard coming out of her place sometimes, on windy nights when the tree branches were scratching my window. The eerie moaning made my hair stand up on my arms and made me bury my head under my pillow to block it out. Sometimes it sounded like a chamber of horrors. But I was so sure it was my imagination playing tricks on me that I didn't even tell anyone. I had my own theories about what was going on in Mrs. Baxter's house, but I preferred to keep them to myself. And I was always sure to keep my distance from that house.

Oh sure. I'd heard the rumours too. I'd seen her myself, standing at her window with binoculars, watching stuff. I'd seen her working in her scraggly little garden out back, tending what looked more like weeds than flowers. And not only did she have about fifty birdhouses and feeders hanging all over her yard, but she also had bat houses. Bat houses! Hanging from posts all over her property.

Sometimes I'd see her sitting in a lawn chair with a little notepad on her lap, scribbling away, completely unmindful to anything that was going on around her. On top of it all, she wore these wild, flowing gowns all the time, and her hair was wild too, all white and fluffy and sticking out in every direction like a dandelion. And she always wore funny red sneakers, instead of the usual "old lady" shoes. But like I said. I kept my mouth shut and my theories trapped inside.

No one was home when Blake and I reached my house. My older sister, Nicki, was in grade ten, and she always hung around after school with her friends. Mom and Dad were at their pet food store, called Contented Pets. They opened it themselves and specialize in a line of organic pet food that's supposed to keep your pet looking and feeling its best. It seems to be working for our animals, too. They must be the healthiest and most well-tended animals in the city. Which is more than I can say for Nicki and me. Mom and Dad spend so much time looking after their store that we've learned to be independent. I'm not complaining. I enjoy it. We even get to help out at the store when the part-time staff can't make it in some weekends and during the holidays. And a little extra cash in your pocket never hurts.

Riley and Otto didn't greet us at the door because they always went to Contented Pets with our parents; one of the benefits of owning their own business was the privilege of taking their dogs to work. But Matilda greeted us with a scolding.

"Dirty bird, dirty bird, dirty bird." She always said that when she was mad.

"Sorry Matilda, but you can't come to school with me," I told her as I handed her a cracker. "You'd talk too much in class."

"I love coming to your house," Blake said, looking around and grinning. "It's so laid-back." He shrugged out of his jacket and backpack and dropped them on the floor alongside all the other stuff that was piled up there. Then he stopped to admire my parents' "wildlife gallery" in the hallway, like he always did. They collect paintings by famous artists, and try to get signed prints, whenever they can. Blake stared at his favourite, the picture of the snowshoe rabbit. He thought it looked like our rabbit, Peter. "So where's this squirrel, anyway?" he finally asked.

"In a cage in the basement," I said, leading him down. I turned on the light and pointed at the cage.

The door was wide open. There was no squirrel in sight.

THREE

"Oh oh," I said.

"What?" Blake asked me. "Where is he?"

"I just remembered something I forgot. Mom asked me to feed him before I went to school this morning. And I did, but...."

"But you forgot to shut the cage door, right Max?"

"Right," I said, and swallowed a huge gulp of dread. "And all the cats in the house were pretty fascinated by that squirrel on the weekend. They watched every move he made. I just hope

he hasn't become cat food." I looked around for the telltale signs of a cat and squirrel ruckus but everything looked normal. Besides, most of the time in our house, it always looks like there's been a ruckus. That's just what normal looks like.

"At least the squirrel's organic, like the food your parents sell," Blake said with a weak grin. I winced.

"Funny," I said. "Now help me find him."

We looked everywhere. Everywhere we could think of looking, anyway. Woody was a baby squirrel, a tiny little thing. He could have been hiding just about anywhere. We checked all the closets and bedrooms, and all the nooks and crannies that might be appealing to a squirrel. We found the kittens curled up in a shoebox, the rabbit under an armchair, the tortoise in a closet, but there was no sign of that squirrel.

Back in the kitchen, when we were drowning our sorrows with milk and cookies, I spotted a message flashing on the answering machine and listened to it.

"Hi, Max." It was Mom's voice, and my milk glass trembled in my hand when I heard it. "We'll be a little late getting home this evening, because we have to unload a shipment that just came in. Put the tuna casserole in the oven at 6:00. Oh, and let Woody out of the cage for some exercise, since he's been cooped up all day. Keep an eye on him too, please. Don't want to lose him in the house! See you soon! Bye." Blake looked at me with wide eyes.

"Well," I said. "At least Woody got plenty of exercise today, didn't he?"

"That's for sure," Blake said. "Maybe a little too much."

Now all I had to do was come up with a good explanation for a missing squirrel by the time my parents got home.

Blake ditched me. He said he had a perfectly good reason for leaving. He said he had guitar lessons at 5:30 and then he had to finish a book report. But he sure didn't waste time getting out of the house long before my parents got home, just in case they showed up early.

Which left me standing in the kitchen, wondering what to do next.

First, I listened, not even sure what I was listening for. What do a squirrel's footsteps sound like? And it's not like they meow or bark or anything, like other animals. I'd heard squirrels making a weird chattering noise from above me in trees before. But at that moment, it was perfectly quiet in our house. Even Matilda was fast asleep with her head tucked under her wing. So I decided I should try to call him.

"Woody," I called. "Woody Squirrel," I called even louder. "Come out, come out wherever you are! I'll give you some nice crunchy sunflower seeds. Maybe even some peanuts! You know how much you like peanuts! Here Woody, Woody, Woody. Pssst. Pssst." I hoped that I was making something like squirrel sounds. "Pssst. Pssst. Pssst." I started clicking my tongue, too, and snapping my fingers, doing anything I could think of to attract Woody's attention without scaring him.

That's when I turned around and saw my sister and her boyfriend, this senior on the football team, standing in the hallway staring at me. The guy had a smirk on his face, and my sister's eyes were wide and disbelieving.

"Max, are you a complete idiot, or what?" Nicki said. It's okay. I'm used to it. That's the way she always talks to me.

"I can't find the squirrel," I told her.

"Then you are a complete idiot," she said. "How could you lose him? What's wrong with you? I brought Dave home to meet him."

I looked over at Dave. He was still smirking.

"Do you always talk to animals, Maximum?" Maximum. He always called me that. Like it was funny or something.

"Yeah," I said. Because they're smarter than big goofs like you, is what I should have added. Except I didn't, because Dave really was big. And a goof. He just stood there, smirking. It was what he did best.

"Well, where's the squirrel?" Nicki kind of shrieked.

"Do you think I'd be acting like this if I knew?" I asked her. "I have no clue where he is. I can't find a trace of him!"

"Maybe the parrot ate it," Dave said. I winced.

"Matilda's not a parrot, she's a cockatoo," I told him. "And she's not like a hawk. She doesn't eat meat. She's a vegetarian."

"Just like our whole family," Nicki added.

"Right," I said. I didn't mention the fact that I was a borderline vegetarian, and nobody else in my family knew about it. If there was meat to be eaten, then I ate it. So I was always trying to find excuses to eat over at Blake's house. They had hamburgers every weekend! Big juicy suckers!

By the time I finished explaining to Nicki how I'd accidentally left the cage door open before school that morning, Dave was howling as he rhymed off everything that might have happened to Woody.

"Or maybe...maybe," he was choking on his laughter, "maybe one of the cats ate it, Maximum! Or maybe it accidentally flushed itself down the toilet. Or...or...got trapped between the walls of the house. Or maybe...." The phone rang, and Dave clammed up. Nicki and I stared at it like it might bite us if we touched it.

"Answer it," she told me.

"What if it's Mom?"

"She's going to find out sooner or later. See if you can stall her. Make something up, Max."

"You're better at that than I am," I reminded her.

"You left the cage door open," she reminded me.

I grabbed the phone. It was Blake. "Guess what? I found your squirrel," he said. "You'd better get over here fast." Then he hung up. I was out the door before Nicki could even ask me who had called.

FOUR

I ran all the way to Blake's house, and didn't even knock when I got there. Blake was sitting at the kitchen table with his chin in his hands, looking pathetic. And something was wrong with that kitchen of his, the one that we always refer to as the operating room. That bright, white, spic-and-span space that never has a trace of dust or crumbs, or even evidence that human beings actually spend time eating there.

There was a broken glass on the ceramic floor, and glass and chocolate milk spattered everywhere. A package of cookies had been torn open and cookie crumbs littered every surface. A couple of herb pots that had once been on the windowsill were tipped over on the floor, and dirt trailed across the room. Every chair was knocked over, every cupboard door was open, every picture on the wall was crooked.

"You're looking at a doomed man," Blake said.

"Where's Woody?"

"I'm not sure. The last time I saw him, he was using the curtains as tree branches, kind of leaping from curtain rod to curtain rod. Then he ran upstairs, and I lost him again."

"But how did he get here in the first place, Blake?"

"He must have stowed away in my pocket. When I got home I hung my coat on the hook in the hall, then went upstairs to do my homework. Next thing I knew, I heard my little sister screaming. She was getting a snack when Woody leaped out of nowhere and landed on the counter. She dropped her glass and hid in the broom closet, and Woody started tearing apart the bag of peanut butter cookies. I tried to catch him, but every time I made a grab, he'd leap out of reach and something else would go flying."

"Where's your mom?" I glanced nervously over my shoulder.

"She volunteers at the seniors' home on Mondays," he said. "She'll be home soon. I am sooo doomed."

"Where's your sister?"

"She took off to her friend's house. She's terrified of that squirrel."

"Let's get this place cleaned up," I said, taking command because Blake was too freaked out to do it himself. "We'll worry about finding Woody when we're done."

We'd just put the vacuum cleaner away and rinsed out the dishcloth when we heard the front door open. Blake's face was so pale he looked like he was about to barf. I nudged him hard in the ribs.

"Relax," I said. "You've got guilt written all over your face."

"But the squirrel...."

"You said he went upstairs. Keep your mom down here, and I'll go up and look around. Hi, Mrs. Mills" I said as she breezed into the kitchen.

"Hi boys," she said. Then she looked around and froze like a deer in head-lights. "What happened here?" she asked.

"Nothing, Mom. That's a weird question. Why would you even ask?" Blake said, maybe a little too quickly.

"Oh my gosh! Look at that! Milk dribbles on the cupboard! Blake, you've

got to be more careful when you're pouring milk, honey." She ruffled his hair, then grabbed the dishcloth and started wiping the chocolate milk spots we'd missed.

That's when I spotted the squirrel. He was sitting in the branches of one of Mrs. Mills' huge tropical plants, watching me, not a metre away from my elbow. I shot out my arm, grabbed him before he could even flick his tail, and tucked him safely into my pocket.

"Well, I've got to go," I said. "Got to put the tuna casserole in the oven soon like my mom asked me!"

I ran all the way home, and kept my hand on that squirming squirrel until I had him safely locked inside the cage. Back in the kitchen, Matilda squawked at me as I put the tuna casserole in the oven. We always gave her a couple of peanuts at suppertime, and it was her way of reminding me.

"Oh, be quiet and wait a minute," I told her. "I've had enough trouble for one day. At least Mom and Dad won't find out about Woody's little adventure, though."

"Woody. Woody. Come out Woody. Come out Woody," Matilda said. "Woody. Woody."

Blackmailed by a bird? I winced, and handed her a peanut.

FIVE

M om! You've got to set him free before he destroys the house!"

My mom was moping in the kitchen, sitting in her favourite chair that faces the bird feeders in the yard. Matilda was on her shoulder, eating sunflower seeds out of her hand. Woody was on her head, kneading her hair.

"But something will happen to him," Mom said. "He can't fend for himself."

"He'll learn," I told her. "He belongs in the wild. We've got to let him loose before he gets too tame."

Woody was starting to shred the curtains, to dig up plants, to chew on furniture. He was ruining stuff, and Mom was in complete denial. I didn't want to remind her about Reggie the raccoon. My parents had found him abandoned a couple of years back, and decided that they would try raising him. It was really neat at first, bottle feeding him, this little ball of fur that liked to curl up on your lap and have a snooze.

But the bigger he got, the harder he was to control. He started chewing on chair legs and raiding the cupboards when our backs were turned. We finally set him free at a nearby ravine, but he came back and began terrorizing the neighbours, raiding garbage cans, scaring people because he wasn't afraid of them and never ran away when they tried to chase him. He even learned to take the screens off windows — he broke into a few houses that way. We weren't very popular on our old street, and I didn't want the same thing to happen on our new one. You just can't keep wild animals as pets! My mom

knew that, too, but she cared so much about the animals that she rescued, she had a tough time making the right decision.

"I don't know," Mom said. "I'll have to talk it over with your dad."

"But it's already been two weeks, Mom. Woody's getting big. You can't wait much longer. Mom?"

She didn't answer me. She just sat there and stared out the window as Matilda nibbled seeds and Woody kneaded her hair.

It was time to take matters into my own hands. I started to devise a little plan. I had to set Woody free, and make it look like an accident. I figured it wouldn't be too tough to let that squirrel scamper outside one day as I was leaving the house. When my parents weren't home, of course. Saturday morning, maybe, when they were busy working at their store, and I could wander around the neighbourhood with Blake, keeping an eye on Woody to make sure he was safe. A fine plan, I figured, and I put it into action as soon as Saturday rolled around!

My sister Nicki was gone to a swimming competition with Dave and I had the house to myself. Blake came over mid-morning, and I told him my plan while he was cuddled up on a chair with Peter Rabbit, stroking his silky fur. Blake loved Peter Rabbit, and all the rest of our pets, but of course, living

in the sterile zone, he could never have a pet of his own.

"Are you crazy?" he said. "Your parents will kill you. They love that squirrel."

"They'll thank me, once they get used to the idea," I said. "Woody is wrecking our house. He's nuts, Blake. We leave him out of the cage more than ever now, because he runs in circles when he's locked inside and he's starting to wear out the fur on his tail. He's got a bald spot! Squirrels need space and freedom to roam, trees and rooftops...."

"Okay, okay, I get your point," Blake said.

"Let's do it, buddy," I said. I only wished that I felt as enthusiastic as I sounded.

Setting him free was easy. He just scooted out the front door when I opened it a crack. Keeping track of him after was a bit harder than I expected, though. The first thing he did was run up a tree and sit there in the warm spring sunshine, flicking his tail.

"Maybe he'll just hang around your house," Blake said. But he spoke too soon.

Woody started doing what squirrels do best. Acrobatics. He leaped from branch to branch until he reached a power line, then zipped across it like a tightrope artist! He managed to keep his balance, even though it was a windy day and the wires were dancing around in the strong gusts.

"Wow. He's good," I said. "Look at him go! Oh oh."

He was headed straight for Mrs. Baxter's house on the squirrel highway above our heads. The power line stretched across our street and connected to a hydro pole on Mrs. Baxter's front lawn. The squirrel reached it in seconds, then sprang into the oak tree on the front lawn, leaped onto the roof of the house, and disappeared over the peak.

"Oh great," I said. "We can't go over there to follow Woody. Nobody goes over there. Ever. Mrs. Baxter's a crazy old hermit."

"A witch," Blake said in a spooky voice. "She's a witch."

"No. A crazy old hermit," I said. I shivered, remembering those groaning sounds that kept me awake some nights. We both stood there for a few minutes, blinking in the bright sunshine and wondering what to do next. "Since Mrs. Baxter's house is on the corner, why don't we just sort of walk along past her yard and see if we can spot Woody," I suggested.

"Whatever you say," Blake said. "It was your idea, so just keep me out of it when your parents start yelling. Okay?"

We wandered along past the hedges that bordered Mrs. Baxter's property, craning our necks as we tried to catch a glimpse of Woody. Then we both spotted him at the same time, and stopped dead in our tracks.

Six

Look at that," Blake murmured. "Maybe she needs a squirrel tail for her witches brew or something, huh Max?"

"Be quiet," I said.

Woody was still in Mrs. Baxter's yard, all right. He was sitting right in the palm of her hand, nibbling sunflower seeds like crazy. And Mrs. Baxter had the biggest smile on her face. She looked up suddenly, and caught us peering at her over the hedge.

"Oh, hello boys," she said. "Look at this tame little squirrel. Isn't he the sweetest thing? And look at his salt-and-pepper fur! How unusual. I wonder where he came from."

Just as I was about to bolt, Blake opened his big mouth.

"His name's Woody," he said. "He actually belongs to my friend Max here."

"Why did you tell her that," I hissed at him.

"Because I figure that if she knows the squirrel has a name, then maybe she won't toss it into her cauldron," he murmured.

"You're crazy," I told him. "She's not a witch."

But when she started to beckon us over with her gnarled fingers, I started to have second thoughts. She sure looked like a witch.

"Come here, boys. I'd like to talk to you for a minute."

Blake's eyes darted towards mine. I shrugged.

"She can't do anything to us in the bright sunshine on a Saturday morning, can she? It's not the right atmosphere."

"Hope not," Blake said.

We didn't walk too quickly. Actually, I was having trouble getting my legs to work at all. They felt as if they had a mind of their own, like they wanted to turn around and run in the other direction.

"How are you?" she said, when we were finally standing in front of her, trembling. Woody was sitting on her shoulder, flicking his tail.

"Good. Real good," I said.

"My name is Alvina Baxter." She stretched out a gnarled hand for us to shake, which we each did a little hesitantly. Her hand felt soft and bony in mine, like I could break it if I squeezed too hard.

We introduced ourselves and she just stood there, smiling at us.

"I'm so glad to finally meet you," she said. "I'm afraid I don't get much of a chance to chat with the neighbours. I'm always so busy, you see. I really should make the time."

Blake and I just stood there staring at her with our mouths clamped shut.

"Well, at least I've met you two now. And your little squirrel. What did you say his name is?"

"Woody. His name's Woody," I said.

"That's a dandy name for a squirrel," Mrs. Baxter said. It made me feel a little better, so then I began to explain how we had a pet squirrel in the first place.

Old Mrs. Baxter stood there smiling the whole time and I started to feel less and less nervous. She wasn't so bad after all. She seemed like somebody's grandmother. A kind of eccentric-looking one, with those crazy sneakers and that wild hair, but still. Maybe she really was somebody's grandmother. Although I'd never seen anyone visiting her. All this was tumbling around in my mind as I spoke to her, so I really didn't hear what she said next. But Blake did, because his eyes had suddenly bugged out.

"Pardon me," I said.

"I was just asking if you boys would mind coming inside for a few minutes. Some nights I hear such strange noises, and I thought maybe you could help me get to the bottom of it."

I looked over at Blake. He was staring at me. His eyes were yelling NO.

"Uh...I...um...." I stammered.

"Come on," she said, leading the way as Woody rode along on her shoulder. "It won't take long."

Blake and I shuffled along behind her. And once again, my legs were desperately trying to convince me to run the other way.

SEVEN

The front door creaked open. Yes, it actually creaked, which made any of the bravery I thought I had take a steep nosedive into my gut. And it was dark in there, even on a bright Saturday morning in April. Maybe it was because of all the dark woodwork, and the heavy curtains that hung on each window. Whatever it was, I was wishing I was back outside, and that Blake hadn't opened his big mouth.

Mrs. Baxter led us down that dark narrow hallway past the dingy living and dining rooms, and through a door. And suddenly I was blinking in bright sunshine. The kitchen was a wide-open space, with windows and skylights and plants, and sketches and paintings hanging everywhere. Nothing at all like the rest of the house. And nothing at all like a witch's house.

"This is where I spend all my time," Mrs. Baxter said. "The house really is too big for me, but I hate to give it up. There are four bedrooms upstairs, but I use one of them as a TV room, and another as a studio. The brightest one. My bedroom, the one that faces the street, is where I hear all those strange sounds. I don't know where they're coming from." She looked distressed when she said that, and clutched her neck with her soft, bony hand.

"What's a studio?" Blake asked.

"Come on up and I'll show you," she said. She led the way back down the hall, with Woody still riding along on her shoulder.

Upstairs she showed us another bright room that I figured was over the kitchen.

"Welcome to my studio," she said.

I couldn't believe my eyes. There was a tilted table by a window, and shelves cluttered with painting supplies. There were a couple of easels in there, too, with wildlife paintings standing on them, some nearly finished, and some only sketches with a few blobs of colour. Mrs. Baxter was a painter! Not a witch or a crazy old hermit. A painter!

"Wow," I said. "This place is so cool. My parents would go crazy in here. They love wildlife paintings. They think it's great to have a signed print. And you're up here painting originals!"

"Are you famous?" Blake asked.

"Not really," Mrs. Baxter said. "I've illustrated a few books, and had shows at some galleries, but I'm not exactly a household name."

"Well, you should be," Blake said.

"It's not as easy as it used to be," she told us. "These old fingers of mine don't work so well any more. It takes me a lot longer to finish a painting these days. But as long as I can hold a paint brush, I'll never stop."

"Amazing," I whispered. I was thinking what an awesome grandmother Mrs. Baxter would make, and actually wishing that she could be mine.

"Now about those noises," she said, and led us into her bedroom.

It was dark in there. The curtains were open, but most of the light was blocked by the thick branches of the towering oak tree on her front lawn. We could see them swaying in the wind like a giant's arms. And that was when we heard it. A low moaning sound that made my hair prickle on the back of my neck. Blake's eyes bugged out again.

"That's it," Mrs. Baxter said. "That's the sound! I usually bury my head under my pillow so I won't hear it. What on earth is it?"

It seemed to be coming from outside, so I ran to the window. I couldn't see anything past those swaying branches. Then I heard it again and I shivered.

"Sounds like someone being tortured, doesn't it?" she said.

She didn't have to tell me that. Those were the same strange sounds that kept me awake some nights. But what was causing them?

"Does this window open, Mrs. Baxter?" I asked.

"Yes," she said. "But it's a tough one. It sticks, so I don't even bother any more. I'm not strong enough."

I yanked it open and stretched my neck out as far as I could. And I spotted it right away — the branch that was causing the problem.

"Look," I yelled triumphantly. "That big branch right there is squeezed up against the one underneath it. Every time the wind blows, they rub together. Listen." As if to prove my point, the wind gusted suddenly, and the tree branches let out that tormented moan. "All you have to do is chop it off, then you'll be able to sleep in peace again." And so will I, I felt like adding.

"Well how will I do that?" she asked, clutching her neck again.

"Don't worry," I told her. "My dad has a chain saw. We'll take care of it for you. As long as you let us burn the wood in our fireplace!"

"Sounds like a deal to me," Mrs. Baxter said. She stretched out her hand and we shook on it. Blake stood there grinning at the two of us. And Woody just crouched comfortably on Mrs. Baxter's shoulder, boldly flicking his tail.

EIGHT

Luckily my parents weren't mad for too long about Woody being on the loose.

In fact, I think my mom was glad that someone, namely me, had made the tough decision for her. My mom is just too softhearted to part with any of the animals that we adopt. Some people would call that a fault. But I think it's one of her better ones! I mean, how bad can it be to care too much about animals?

The one problem I never considered when I let Woody bolt through the front door that day, was how comfortable he felt around humans. Just because he was free, didn't mean that he wanted to run away.

Oh sure, he loved having the freedom to climb through trees, scurry along wires and play tag with the other squirrels on our street. But since he'd been raised with people, he had absolutely no fear of them. He was probably mixed up, wasn't sure if he was one of them or one of us!

I also think Woody figured that every person had a pocket, and that every pocket had a peanut.

Blake and I were out shooting hoops in front of my garage after school when it happened for the first time.

"Look who's coming," Blake told me between bounces. I turned to look in the direction he was pointing. It was my favourite person.

"What's he doing here," I groaned. "Nicki isn't even home."

"Hey Maximum," Dave called as he loped along the street in his long football-player stride, his hands tucked deep in his pockets. "Where's your sister?"

"She's not home," I yelled back, hoping he'd turn around and head in the other direction. He lived just around the corner, which was way too close for comfort, in my opinion. "She's working on a project at the library. She won't be back for an hour."

"Oh yeah? Mind if I wait around for her? I'll teach you two scrawny shrimps a few things about basketball."

Great. That was the last thing I wanted to hear.

"That's okay, Dave. Blake and I are just about done."

"Yeah," Blake added. "I've got to get home for supper."

Dave snatched the ball from Blake in mid-bounce.

"Oh, afraid I'll clean up, huh?" He started to spin it on his finger, spin it and spin it until it was an orange blur, just like I did sometimes with the globe in my classroom. "Well, you're probably right. Nobody's a match for Brave Dave, on the basketball court, the football field or the hockey rink. I'm telling you dudes, I'm MVP every year!"

Then he started bouncing the ball, under his leg, behind his back, lunging and pivoting and dunking, the biggest show-off in the world. And we stood there watching him with our mouths hanging open, probably even drooling.

As Brave Dave was demonstrating his athletic brilliance, I spotted Woody creeping slowly along the driveway behind him. I gave Blake the slightest nudge, and he nudged me right back.

Bounce, pivot, dunk. "And I'm practically double your height and weight. So I guess I can understand if you're too wimpy to go a few rounds with me, even with a two on one advantage...."

And those were the last boastful words that came out of

Dave's mouth. Because right in the middle of crowing his heroics at us, Woody took a flying leap and landed halfway up his pant leg!

"Aaaargh!!!" Dave screamed. He started shaking his leg like there was a rattlesnake attached to him instead of a curious baby squirrel. "Get it off! Hurry up! Aaaargh! Get it off before it bites me and gives me rabies!!! Help!"

"Boy," Blake said. "His mouth is even bigger when he's screaming than it is when he's bragging."

"Need some help there, Brave Dave?" I yelled over Dave's panicky screams. "Or are you tough enough to handle a baby squirrel by yourself?"

"Just get the crazy thing off me, you jerk!"

"I plucked Woody off Dave's pant leg and tucked him in my coat pocket where there were plenty of peanuts to keep him out of trouble for a while. Dave scowled at both of us then spun around and went slinking down the street with his tail between his legs.

"Nice work, Woody." I peeked into my pocket at the squirming squirrel. "Brave Dave probably won't be calling me Maximum any more. What do you think, Blake?"

Blake gave me a high five, and we both stood there grinning.

And it did seem hilarious at the time, and we did laugh about it at school the next day, and blabber on about it to anybody who would listen. And Woody did come across as the big hero. But everything started to fall apart right after that, when I got home from school that same afternoon.

I was still chuckling all the way down the street as I approached the scene of yesterday's crime on our driveway. I kept imagining the stunned look on Brave Dave's face, the way he was dancing around trying to shake Woody off his leg. And the way he went creeping home dragging his bruised ego behind him. He hadn't even called our house to talk to Nicki last night, so now she was mad at him. Guess he was afraid that I'd answer the phone. Hee hee!!

I passed one of the neighbours working in his garden.

"Hi Mr. McGowan," I called, and waved at him. He waved right back.

As I headed towards my house, scanning the treetops and bushes for the furry "suspect," I heard a shout from behind me.

"Hey! What do you think you're doing, tree-rat?"

I thought he was talking to me, so I turned around.

Mr. McGowan was walking backwards across his lawn. He was pointing his garden hose at something. That something was Woody.

"Back off, tree-rat. Back off, or I'll let you have it!"

But Woody wasn't backing off. He was stalking boldly towards Mr. McGowan, who was wearing some sort of gardening apron that had huge pockets.

Oh oh, I thought. Not again! Then I started to run.

"Hold it, Mr. McGowan. That's my squirrel," I yelled. "Don't worry, he won't hurt you. He's just looking for a peanut."

Too late. Once again, Woody took his famous flying leap, and landed right on the gardening apron.

"Yikes! Where did you come from, you bold little rodent! Get away from me." He shook his apron and Woody hit the ground running. Then he went after him with the hose, shooting an arc of icy spray through the air. I scooped Woody up, dropped him in my pocket and dashed for my backyard before a drop of water ever touched him.

NINE

The next weekend, first thing Saturday morning, my dad and I chopped Mrs. Baxter's groaning tree branch down without any problems. She was so grateful, she couldn't stop thanking us. She even baked a banana loaf, and delivered it to our door Saturday afternoon when I was the only one home. When I heard the doorbell, I jumped; I was reading a mystery novel for a book report, and I was at a really scary part. Before I answered I peered out, not because I was afraid of who might be standing there, but because I'm not too crazy about letting people into our house. Especially my friends. Like I said before, Blake's the only one who really understands about the mess.

When I saw Mrs. Baxter standing there with a foil-wrapped plate in her hands, I hesitated for a second. She hadn't been inside our house yet, and I wasn't sure if I was ready to let her see the cluttered muddle that we lived in. Or get a whiff of it. So I only opened the door a crack.

"Hi there, Mrs. Baxter," I said.

"Hello, Max." She paused for a moment, like she was waiting for the invitation that I didn't plan on offering. "Aren't you going to let me in?"

"Um..." I said, just as she edged her way inside. I started to babble out an explanation, right away, just like I always do. "Sorry about the mess. My parents are so busy with their pet shop, and their nature hikes, and all their environmental protection groups, and we have so many animals living here, and my sister and I try to help as much as we can, but, well, sometimes we just don't get around to keeping things too tidy."

"No need to explain," she told me. "I heard a saying once, and those are the words I live by. A creative mess is better than idle tidiness. It looks like your family lives by those words, too. You should be proud, not ashamed."

"I never really thought of it that way," I said.

She handed me the plate. "Banana bread," she said. "Still warm. Why don't you have a piece right now."

"I think I will," I told her. "Why don't you come in for a cup of tea."

"I think I will," she told me. "And maybe I'll have a slice of that banana bread myself. My gosh! You have a cockatoo. I love them!"

"Dirty bird," Matilda said, and Mrs. Baxter walked right over to chat with her.

Half an hour later nearly half the loaf was gone. I had devoured it all myself. Mrs. Baxter only had one little slice. We were talking about Woody and having a few chuckles. And when I told her the story of Brave Dave, she laughed out loud.

"He loves being free," I told her. "And he thinks he owns this neighbourhood. He's eating peanuts out of little kids' hands, climbing up screen doors and begging for food. He thinks that every pocket has a peanut, I'm sure! Yesterday he jumped right up on Mr. McGowan when he was out working in his garden!

"Hmm," Mrs. Baxter said. "Did Mr. McGowan seem to mind?"
"I'm not sure. I think he was a bit shocked. He shook Woody off, then chased him with the hose."

"But was he laughing? Or did he seem angry?" Mrs. Baxter said. She looked serious all of a sudden, and I started to feel uneasy.

"Um," I said. "Well, he was kind of yelling, calling Woody a tree-rat. I rescued him, and shoved him right into my pocket. As I was running for home, Mr. McGowan told me to keep my squirrel off his property. But how am I supposed to do that?"

"I hope he doesn't try to get involved," she said.

"What do you mean?" I asked her.

"I mean by registering a complaint. You know how nervous people get about animals that are behaving strangely. They worry about rabies and things like that. Mr. McGowan might be genuinely concerned."

I gulped. Memories of Reggie the raccoon came flooding back. Memories of all the crazy things he did before the pest control company finally trapped him and took him away. Memories of how upset my mom was, because we never did find out what they did with him, where they released him, if they even did. I didn't want her to go through something like that again, worrying that one of her hand-raised animals was going to be put to sleep. All those thoughts were clambering around in my head just like Woody clambers around in trees, when the doorbell rang again. For some reason my stomach twisted into a knot.

I stood up slowly and shuffled to the door. I peered out through the curtain. There was a man in a uniform standing there. The crest on his shirt said Critter Ridders. And even worse, I recognized him. He'd been to our house before, when we lived in our old neighbourhood. He was the one who'd trapped Reggie raccoon and taken him away forever. The same guy! I gulped again.

"Looks like we didn't move far enough away," I murmured.

TEN

My first impulse was not to answer. Maybe if I didn't open the door, he'd think that nobody was home and he'd leave.

"Who is it?" Mrs. Baxter said. "Why don't you answer, Max?"

I took a few steps back so the guy at the door wouldn't hear. "It's the pest control company," I told her. "I'm afraid to answer. He's probably looking for Woody."

"Would you like me to do it?"

"I'd love that," I said, then sidled into the next room.

Just before Mrs. Baxter opened the door she mussed up her tousled hair a little more, then hunched over like she had a bad back. She turned around and winked at me.

"It's my 'old lady' routine," she whispered. "It works every time. Just watch!" Then she opened the door. "Can I help you, dear," she said to the Critter Ridders man.

"Sorry to bother you, ma'am, but I'm looking for Mr. and Mrs. Harper," he said.

"Pardon me?" She put her hand to her ear and I had to stifle a laugh behind my hand. "I can't hear too well."

"Mr. and Mrs. Harper. Do they live here?"

"Well, I'm pretty sure they do. But they're not here right now, I'm afraid. Is there anything I can help you with, dear?"

"Someone called us about a crazy squirrel that's terrifying people in the neighbourhood, and we were told that it lives here."

Terrifying? What could possibly be terrifying about a baby squirrel? That's what I wanted to blurt out from my hiding spot, but I kept my lips zipped.

"Oh, I don't know about that. I haven't seen any squirrels in this house. There's plenty outside. Don't know if they're crazy, though." I had to bite my tongue to keep from laughing out loud!

"You're sure about that," the guy said. "You're sure there aren't any squirrels being kept as pets in this house that might have gotten outside?" He tried to peek over her shoulder into the rest of the room, like there might be crazy squirrels lurking in every corner, poised for attack.

"I think I know what a squirrel looks like, young man. And unless that cockatoo in the cage over there is wearing a disguise, then, yes, I'm pretty darn sure of it! No squirrels here!"

"Dirty bird! Dirty bird!" Matilda said.

The Critter Ridders guy took a step back, like he was afraid Mrs. Baxter was going to slug him or something. By then, that laugh was fighting so hard with my lips to get out, I was sure it was going to escape any second.

"Well then, I guess you can't help me after all," the guy said. "Thanks for your time though."

"What's that, dear?" Mrs. Baxter said, putting her hand up to her ear again.

"Never mind," he said.

I watched out the window as he walked away shaking his head. When Mrs. Baxter shut the door, the laugh that I'd been trying to swallow finally exploded out of my mouth. She straightened up and tucked her hair back into place.

"Sad, isn't it, how annoyed and impatient some people get with old folks?"

"You're pretty good at faking old, Mrs. Baxter," I told her.

"I wasn't really faking it," she said. "I was just exaggerating, adding some extra quirks for effect! I think we've stalled him for a while, Max. But you'd better come up with a plan soon if you want to save your squirrel!"

I did come up with a plan, and it was a good one, too. But I didn't have the heart to put it into action because I knew how much it would upset my mom. I told Blake all about it when we were walking home from the bus stop after school on Monday afternoon.

"If we don't want the same thing that happened to Reggie the raccoon to happen to Woody the squirrel, then we're going to have to catch Woody ourselves and release him somewhere far from here, where he can't ever find us again," I explained. "That way he'll be safe from that pest control company."

"That shouldn't be too hard," Blake said. "You've just got to catch him and put him in the cage again. Remember the other day when that man was spraying Woody with the hose, he climbed right into your pocket!"

"Not as easy as you'd think, Blake. Woody only gets caught when he wants to get caught. I tried it yesterday, and I couldn't grab hold of him. He'd let me get close enough, then scramble up a tree out of reach. He's pretty tricky."

"So what's your plan?" Blake said.

"That's why I asked you over here after school." I gave him a little nudge with my elbow. "I thought you'd be able to help me."

"The squirrel likes Mrs. Baxter, right? He even eats out of her hand. Maybe Mrs. B. might be able to help us catch Woody," Blake suggested.

"Maybe," I said. "But he's gotten really skittish lately. I think he's afraid of getting caught. He'll eat calmly out of your hand, but if you try to pat him, he jumps right out of reach." I kicked a stone on the sidewalk and watched it bounce and roll ahead of me. "Even Mrs. Baxter's magic touch with Woody might not work any more."

Just then Blake gave me a little nudge with his elbow.

"Look," he said, pointing in the direction of my house. There was a white van parked on the street with a telltale amber bubble-light on top. Right away I knew it was the pest control truck, with those reinforced mesh windows on the back doors. And right away I knew we were in trouble.

"Nuts," I said. I leaned against Blake and steered him towards Mrs. Baxter's side yard, which we were just passing. "Duck down in here," I told him.

The same guy in his goofy uniform was standing on our front lawn, talking to my mom. Her voice was high, and kind of shrieking. I could hear every word she was saying and she didn't sound too thrilled.

"The last time you took away one of our animals, our raccoon that we had so lovingly nurtured after finding him abandoned, you couldn't tell us what became of him," she said. Or shrieked. "I know your job is important, and you're actually taking the animal's well-being into consideration, but I really care about all the animals that we hand raise in this house, and I'd prefer to deal with the problem myself!"

"I'm sorry, Ma'am. But you're going to have to let me catch this squirrel. Someone has hired me to do this job. And besides, your neighbours are afraid of it."

"But he's harmless. He's not the least bit dangerous."

"I still have to do my job, Ma'am," he said.

"We'll see about that," Mom said. She spun around, stomped into the house and slammed the door. The Critter Ridder started walking slowly towards his van.

"Whoa! She's mad," Blake said.

"Don't fool yourself," I told him. "She's probably curled up on a chair, crying or something. She's not as tough as she sounds."

"Well, at least she's held him off for a while. Looks like he's leaving."

"Yeah," I agreed. "Probably got scared when she started shouting. I know I do! Wait a minute. What's the guy doing now?"

He had the back doors of the van open. He was leaning inside, hauling out a box trap and a net on a long pole. Then he turned around and started scanning the trees!

Oh no! He thinks he's going to catch Woody right now!" Blake said.

"And he just might." I told him. "Woody always hangs around when I get home from school and scrounges for the peanuts I carry in my pocket. And he's easy to identify because of those grey and white markings, so the guy can't possibly mistake another squirrel for ours. We've got to catch Woody first!"

"What's wrong, boys?"

We both turned around at the same time. Mrs. Baxter was standing behind us, and I pointed at the scene across the road. "Looks like trouble is brewing," she said.

"Big time," I told her. "We've got to catch Woody before he does." "Well, it looks like you might have your chance, because here comes the dangerous suspect right now," Mrs. Baxter said.

And sure enough, there was Woody, strutting along the street in that cheeky way of his, headed right towards Mrs. Baxter's front yard. The pest control guy spotted him at the same instant that we did.

He started to creep towards the squirrel, holding out that long net of his. I knew that any sudden move would scare him and he'd bolt for the nearest tree. I also knew that if Blake and I didn't do something fast, we'd never see Woody again.

"Come on, Blake. Let's get to work," I said. We both leaped out from behind the bushes to startle Woody, and he went skittering halfway up the hydro pole on Mrs. Baxter's lawn.

"Hey! What are you doing?" the guy said. He shook his net at us. "I'm trying to trap that squirrel. It's a menace to this neighbourhood."

"How do you know that's the right squirrel, Mr. Critter Ridder?" I challenged him. "How can you be so sure?"

"Because its colour fits the description. And look how bold the thing is! It has no fear of humans!"

Woody was clinging to the pole, flicking his tail and scolding us. He was so low that the pest control guy thought he might be able to snag that so-called crazy squirrel in his net, right then and there. Slowly, carefully, he edged closer so Woody wouldn't get startled away again.

"Woody! Beat it!" I hollered. Blake and I clapped our hands loudly to chase him away.

It worked. Woody sprang through the air, landed right on the guy's head, scrambled down his arm and reached the ground before he even knew what had happened. Then he dashed across the lawn, made another leap and sailed into some thick vines that clung to the brick walls of Mrs. Baxter's house. Frightened sparrows nesting in the vines flew in angry circles as Woody climbed higher. In a moment he was perched on the rooftop, where he squatted, scolded us again, then clambered over the top and disappeared.

"And that," I said to the pest control guy, who stood with his mouth hanging open, staring at the rooftop, "is the last we'll see of Woody the squirrel for a while. I don't really think he wants to be locked up in a cage. Would you? He's probably gone off to hide somewhere. And sorry, sir, but like my mom said, we'd rather take care of the problem our own way."

I really did feel sorry for Mr. Critter Ridder. After all, he was just trying to do his job. He waited around for a few minutes, in case Woody showed up again, pacing back and forth in front of Mrs. Baxter's house and shooting us these angry scowls.

By the time he finally gave up and began to load his equipment back into the van, he was wearing a major frown. Just before he got inside, he took one last look around. That's when Mrs. Baxter came doddering across her lawn. She was doing her 'old lady' routine again, and I nudged Blake in the ribs.

"Watch this," I said.

"Oh, hello again, dear," she said. "I see you're back. Did you find any of those crazy squirrels you were looking for the other day?"

"There's only one," he said. "And I found it. But these two boys here scared it off before I had a chance to trap it." He shot us another nasty scowl, and we both looked down at our shoes.

"Oh dear. What a shame." Mrs. Baxter clicked her tongue sympathetically. "That must be one clever squirrel, to out-smart a professional like you."

He raised his eyebrows and stared at her. "Don't worry. I'll catch it when I come back tomorrow," he warned us just before he slammed the van door and drove away.

"Nice work," Blake said as he shook my hand.

"Yeah," I said. "Now, if we can only find Woody again before he does."

"Well, that shouldn't be too much of a problem," Mrs. Baxter said. As she watched the van disappear around the corner, she reached into her sweater pocket and pulled out a squirming bundle of fur. "He knows I always carry sunflower seeds in my pocket. He hopped right in when he found me in the yard a few minutes ago!"

Blake and I stood there grinning as we scratched Woody between the ears while he nibbled away on the seeds.

TWELVE

We moved Woody to his new home that very night. We chose a park on the outskirts of the city, certain that he'd never be able to find us again. Mom knew it was the best thing to do, but as we watched the squirrel go skittering away, she had tears in her eyes.

"He was such a sweet little thing," Mom said, and Dad wrapped an arm around her shoulder and squeezed.

"And I'm sure there will be plenty more wild animals for you to nurture, before too long," he told her. "So cheer up."

"You know we had to do this, Mom," I reminded her as we watched Woody exploring an oak tree in his shady forest home. "See, he's already hunting for acorns! He'll be just fine." I grabbed my mom's hand to show my support.

"I realize that now, Max. Thanks for helping out," she said, and gave my hand a hard squeeze.

Later that evening we were sitting in the kitchen finishing off the last of Mrs. Baxter's banana bread with mugs of hot chocolate when there was a knock at the door. When I opened it, Mrs. Baxter was standing there. She had a package under her arm.

"How's your Mom?" she whispered to me. "Is she feeling any better?"

"A little," I told her.

"Well, I've got something that might just cheer her up," Mrs. Baxter said.

"Come on in." As I opened the door for her, I took a quick glance at the jumbled mess that was normal in our house. A comfortable mess, I thought. "And don't forget...a creative mess is better than idle tidiness. Right, Mrs. Baxter?"

"You said it," she agreed with a wink.

Mom was all befuddled when Mrs. Baxter presented her with the package that was wrapped in brown paper.

"What's this?" she asked, all grinning and curious. It was nice to see her smiling.

"Just a little something," Mrs. Baxter said mysteriously. "I hope you

like it. I had to rush a bit to get it done on time. But I wanted you to have it today."

Mom looked perplexed as she unwrapped the package, and Dad leaned forward expectantly. Then they both gasped.

"It's beautiful," Mom said. "It looks exactly like Woody! Where did you get this?"
She was holding a water-colour painting of a squirrel nibbling sunflower seeds. It looked exactly like Woody, right down to the salt-and-pepper fur and cheeky sparkling eyes. It was amazing.

"Well, I painted it, of course. Didn't Max tell you that I'm a painter?"

"No! He didn't tell us!" She glanced over at me and frowned. "How could you forget something like that, Max?"

I shrugged. "I guess I was too worried about Woody," I said.

"You painted this yourself?" Mom still couldn't believe it. Then she looked at the signature on the bottom. "A.V. Baxter. Don't tell me that you're the real Alvina Violet Baxter? I buy greeting cards with your paintings on them all the time. This is incredible! Thank you so much. This looks exactly like Woody!"

"Well it should," she said. "I took a photo of him while he was gobbling seeds from one of my bird feeders last week. Bold little thing!"

"Where should we hang it?" Dad said, glancing around the room.

"We've got to display it in a place of honour."

And that's just what we did. We hung it in the kitchen, on the wall right above the table, where we can see it all the time. Whenever I look at it, I wonder about Woody, about how he's doing in his new home at the park where he's safe to wander and explore without getting into trouble. Sometimes I wish he'd come back for a visit. In fact, I'm always on the lookout for a squirrel with salt-and-pepper fur like Woody's. I even carry peanuts around in my pocket all the time, just in case!

BIOGRAPHIES

Toronto author DEB LOUGHEAD has been writing ever since she learned how to read. After graduating from the University of Toronto, she worked briefly as a catalogue copy editor. Then, in 1981, Deb decided to stay at home to raise her family, three sons who have always provided inspiration and a receptive ear. In the early 1980s she became involved with Etobicoke's *Spires Magazine*. For 15 years she was an associate editor, writing short stories, poetry, and articles for the children's pages.

Deb's poetry and fiction, for both children and adults, have appeared in a variety of publications across the country. She enjoys visiting classrooms to conduct workshops and storytelling sessions. *A Pocketful of Fur* is her fifth children's book.

The Yelling Birke Sister (AKA Lisa Birke) was born in 1976 in the Bavarian Alps. She immigrated to Canada in her early childhood with her family and lived in Shawnigan Lake until 1994. She graduated from the Emily Carr Institute of Art and Design in 1999. Lisa shares a house in Burnaby with other yelling Birke sister and a squealing guinea pig by the name of Babalu. Lisa exhibits with the Bau-Xi Gallery in Vancouver and Toronto, and has also had shows of paintings and sculptural work at One Hundred Mile House, the Osoyoos Art Gallery, and the Luft Gallery in Toronto. She loves cookies, ice cream and stinky fruit.